KIM

LOST

WORDS

Unveiling the Dark Secrets of Hollywood's Power, Betrayal, and Deception

Robert Carter

Table of Content

Introduction

Hollywood has always been seen as the land of dreams: an industry where aspirations are transformed into reality, building myths and legends that transcend generations. But behind the sparkle of the stars, there's a dark side of power, silence, and abuse. The scandal involving Sean "Diddy" Combs and his former partner Kim Porter has shattered this polished facade, revealing an industry that, beneath the surface, hides unspoken secrets.

Why are these revelations so important?

Kim Porter, an icon of beauty and style, lived in the shadow of one of the most powerful figures in music and entertainment. Her tragic passing in 2018 left not only an emotional void for her loved ones, but also a silence that, over time, has grown louder. Kim's personal diaries, which surfaced after her death, tell a story that goes beyond Hollywood gossip. They reveal the reality of a woman trapped in a cycle of abuse, secrets that are now coming to light, and questions that force us to confront what we truly know about our idols.

Diddy's arrest in 2024 on serious charges like sex trafficking and abuse was a turning point in this public drama. The revelations contained in Kim Porter's diaries seem to have acted as a catalyst for these accusations, reviving old stories of power abuse, manipulation, and systemic injustices within one of the world's most influential industries.

The Role of the #MeToo Movement

This scandal is part of a broader context—the #MeToo movement, which shook Hollywood and other industries at the end of 2017. Since then, many celebrities have faced similar accusations, and Diddy's case is no exception. It proves that change is underway and that the voices of victims can no longer be silenced. The culture of silence, which has allowed powerful figures to abuse their status for decades, is slowly crumbling, and this case is a glaring example.

The Power of Kim Porter's Diaries

At the heart of this book are those diaries. Private words, thoughts Kim never imagined would be made public, are now serving as key evidence in an investigation that could forever alter the public's perception of Diddy and, by extension, Hollywood itself. But this isn't just a story of abuse. These diaries stand as a tribute to a woman who sought justice even in silence — a figure who suffered behind the scenes of a life that seemed perfect. They are a testament to resilience, struggle, and, ultimately, hope for those who believe the truth will emerge.

Why is this book necessary?

In a historical moment when the line between reality and fiction feels more blurred than ever, the Diddy-Porter case forces us to confront uncomfortable truths. This isn't just a story of power and abuse; it's a reflection on the nature of the entertainment industry — how people's lives are manipulated for public pleasure, and how, too often, justice is denied to those without a voice. This book not only recounts the facts but seeks to go beyond, exploring how and why we arrived at this point.

In the following pages, we will explore not only the specific case of Sean "Diddy" Combs but also the broader context in which these accusations sit. We will talk about Kim Porter, not just as a victim, but as a complex figure who tried to navigate a world where power corrupts, and money often obscures the truth. This book is a call to action: to reflect, discuss, and, most importantly, change the way we view the world behind Hollywood's lights.

Chapter 1: The Portrait of Kim Porter

The Beginning: The Rise of an Extraordinary Woman

Kimberly Porter, born on December 16, 1970, in Columbus, Georgia, was a woman with far more to offer than the public image of a celebrity's partner. Raised with a dream to break into the entertainment world, Kim was driven by an unshakable ambition and determination. She wasn't just a model; she was a woman who envisioned building a career that would make her a significant figure in the world of entertainment. Though she is often remembered for her relationship with Sean "Diddy" Combs, her professional journey began long before they met.

Kim moved to New York in the early 1990s, seeking opportunities to establish herself in the entertainment industry. During those years, she posed for some of the most influential fashion magazines and appeared in various music videos—a common stepping stone for many models at the time. Her magnetic presence and natural charm quickly made her a recognized figure in the entertainment scene. But what always set Kim apart from others in the industry was her vision of herself as more than just an image: she wanted to create, produce, and influence.

Meeting Diddy: Love, Allure, and Compromises

In 1994, Kim's life changed drastically when she met Sean "Diddy" Combs, then one of the most powerful and influential music producers in the recording industry. What began as a professional collaboration soon evolved into a romantic relationship that would define their lives for over a decade. Diddy, known for his charisma and entrepreneurial talent, offered Kim not only a life of luxury and opportunities but also a platform that placed her in the center of media attention.

However, their relationship — seemingly perfect to the public — was far more complicated and tumultuous behind the scenes. The pressure of being the partner of one of the world's biggest entertainment stars was not easy to manage. Diddy's infidelities, the constant spotlight on their private life, and the demands of being a full-time mother to three children led Kim to sacrifice much of her own career in the interest of family stability.

Despite everything, Kim always strived to maintain a sense of independence. "I don't want to be just a side figure in his life," she reportedly told close friends. Even though her professional ambitions were often overshadowed by Diddy's fame, Kim continuously sought to maintain her own identity.

Her Private Life: Between Love and Suffering

Behind the appearances of luxury and glamour, Kim's life was filled with moments of profound suffering. The diaries she left behind after her death reveal shocking details about what occurred behind closed doors. Years of emotional abuse, betrayals, and manipulations left deep scars. While rumors of crisis in their relationship were well known, few had imagined the full extent of Kim's private torment.

In 2007, the couple briefly separated after Kim discovered yet another of Diddy's infidelities, which had resulted in a child with another woman. Nevertheless, despite their official separation, the two remained closely bonded, often reconciling. "We're like magnets," Kim once said in an interview. "Even when we pull apart, something always brings us back together."

However, the diaries—brought to light only after her death—reveal that behind these reconciliations was much more than just mutual attraction. Kim was trapped in a cycle of abuse and emotional dependency. Her writings describe a woman who fought to break free from Diddy's shadow but found it nearly impossible to escape his control. Life with Diddy was not just made of exclusive parties and red carpets but also moments of deep loneliness and anguish.

The Discovery of the Diaries: Truth Beyond Death

Kim Porter's sudden death in November 2018 shocked Hollywood. Initially attributed to complications from pneumonia, her passing raised many questions. However, only years later, when her diaries were uncovered, did the true picture of her life begin to emerge in stark and dramatic clarity. The words she had written in private, kept even from her closest friends, told a story of pain and resilience that no one had imagined.

These diaries were not merely a record of Kim's personal suffering but a testament to the complexity of her life. Kim was not just a victim but a woman constantly striving to reconcile her love for Diddy with her need to protect herself and her children. The pages contain episodes of emotional and physical abuse that cast a dark shadow over her relationship with Diddy, and which now play a central role in the legal charges against him.

What makes these diaries even more significant is that they represent the voice of a woman who, despite her public silence, desperately sought to be heard. Her words are not just a cry of pain but an act of courage and truth. Kim knew that one day, these pages might make a difference, and now they are playing a crucial role in bringing to light a story of abuse and injustice.

Kim Porter: A Life of Strength and Fragility

The figure of Kim Porter is filled with complexity. Despite everything she endured, she remains a symbol of strength for many women. Those who knew her describe her as a devoted mother — a woman who, despite her personal struggles, always sought to protect her children and ensure them a safe future. Her diaries reveal a woman acutely aware of her own limits but also incredibly resilient.

Kim was never someone who publicly complained about her difficulties. She always maintained a facade of composure and dignity, trying to keep her private life out of the spotlight, even when the weight of that life became unbearable. However, with the publication of her writings, the world has finally been able to see the reality behind that facade — a brave but vulnerable woman who fought until the end for her dignity.

Chapter 2: The Relationship with Sean "Diddy" Combs – Between Love and Power

A Love Story Under the Spotlight

The relationship between Kim Porter and Sean "Diddy" Combs was one of the most followed and discussed throughout the '90s and early 2000s. From the public's perspective, it seemed to embody the dream of a power couple: him, a music mogul, successful producer, and visionary entrepreneur; her, a captivating model and the mother of their children. But behind the glamorous facade of public appearances, interviews, and photoshoots, lay a relationship marked by power dynamics, emotional conflict, and forms of abuse that would only come to light years later.

The Beginning of Their Relationship

Kim met Sean Combs in the early '90s when both were still on the rise in their respective careers. Diddy, already known for his talent in discovering new artists in the music industry, was captivated by Kim's beauty and strong personality. Although they were initially just friends, their connection quickly grew, turning into a passionate romantic relationship. But from the start, their relationship was complicated.

Diddy was already known for his relentless ambition and dominant personality — two traits that would deeply shape his personal life. Kim, on the other hand, was an independent woman trying to make a name for herself in the entertainment world. Their love story, while filled with moments of great affection, was also marked by turbulence, separations, and reconciliations.

Love and Control: A Tormented Relationship

At the height of their relationship, Diddy and Kim seemed like a happy, fulfilled couple. They attended exclusive events together, raised a family, and often shared public displays of tenderness. However, as revealed in Kim's diaries, behind those perfect images lay a very different reality.

One of the most disturbing aspects revealed in the diaries is the control Diddy exerted over Kim. This control wasn't just emotional but also material. Diddy, with his immense wealth and influence, controlled every aspect of Kim's life, from her career decisions to her personal choices. This power imbalance manifested in many of their interactions, with Kim at times describing their relationship as "a constant struggle to find space to breathe."

Diddy's reputation for being demanding and tough was well known even in his early career. He had earned a reputation as someone who expected nothing less than total control over everything in his orbit. This authoritarian personality extended to his personal relationships. Kim, who was initially charmed by Diddy's charisma and energy, soon found herself struggling to maintain a sense of self within the relationship.

Infidelity and Betrayal: The Cost of Fame

One of the recurring themes in Kim Porter's diaries is the pain caused by Diddy's numerous infidelities. Their relationship was characterized by periods of separation and reconciliation, often driven by his betrayals. The most infamous case was the birth of a daughter from another relationship in 2007 — a turning point that deeply hurt Kim and led to a temporary split. Yet, despite everything, their bond seemed unbreakable. Kim, even while aware of Diddy's infidelities, seemed unable to distance herself from him completely.

In her diary, Kim frequently described the humiliation and betrayal she felt each time she discovered Diddy's new affairs. But what hurt her most wasn't just the affairs themselves, but the way Diddy would justify his actions — minimizing her pain and belittling her emotions. This kind of manipulation, often present in abusive relationships, made Kim increasingly insecure and dependent on her partner.

Diddy's infidelities weren't just personal affronts to Kim—they were also a form of psychological abuse. He knew that each betrayal would weaken her further, strengthening his control over her. The way Diddy handled these situations—often downplaying the impact of his actions—created an environment in which Kim felt increasingly vulnerable and lost.

Their Children: A Bond That Couldn't Be Broken

Despite their personal struggles, Diddy and Kim shared a deep love for their children. Together, they had three kids: Christian, born in 1998, and twin daughters D'Lila Star and Jessie James, born in 2006. Kim also had a son from a previous relationship, Quincy, whom Diddy treated as his own.

Kim was a devoted mother, and much of her energy was dedicated to ensuring that her children grew up in a loving and protected environment, despite the turbulence of her personal life. In her diaries, it is clear that the children were the main reason Kim tried to maintain a civil relationship with Diddy, even during the hardest times. "For them," she wrote in one entry, "I have to be strong. I have to do whatever it takes to protect them."

A Love That Couldn't Be Broken

What makes Kim and Diddy's relationship so complex is the deep emotional bond that, despite everything, continued to connect them. Even in their worst moments, Kim admitted multiple times in her writings that she couldn't help but love Diddy. There was an almost magnetic attraction between them — a connection that went beyond mere romantic love. This bond, nurtured by years of shared experiences and a profound sense of mutual belonging, made it difficult for Kim to find the strength to leave him for good.

For his part, Diddy has always spoken of Kim with great affection, even after their separations. In an interview after Kim's death, Diddy said, "She was the love of my life. No matter what happened between us, she will always be my soulmate." However, the rhetoric of eternal love could not erase the pain that Kim had endured over the years.

The Fight for Autonomy

In the final years of her life, Kim began seeking emotional and professional independence from Diddy. Even though they continued to see each other and maintained a cordial relationship for the sake of their children, Kim sought to rebuild her identity outside of Diddy's shadow. She wanted to revive her modeling career and explore new opportunities in the entertainment world. However, as her diaries reveal, every attempt at emancipation seemed to be sabotaged by Diddy's persistent control over her life.

In her later years, Kim became increasingly focused on her family and her personal projects, striving to create a space for herself and her children away from the toxic dynamics that had characterized much of her life with Diddy. Unfortunately, fate did not allow her to live long enough to see all of her dreams of independence fully realized.

Chapter 3: The Accusations Revealed

Breaking the Silence: The Beginning of the Scandal

Kim Porter's life, marked by years of a tumultuous relationship with Sean "Diddy" Combs, had been wrapped in silence — until her tragic death in 2018, which shattered that silence with the discovery of her personal diaries. In these intimate pages, hidden and perhaps never intended to be read, Kim told a story of emotional and physical abuse, manipulation, and control that now sits at the heart of the allegations against Diddy.

These revelations were not only shocking but also unleashed a media storm, casting a dark shadow over one of the most powerful men in the music industry. The accusations of abuse against Diddy, long confined to whispers and rumors, have now become part of an official investigation, creating one of the biggest scandals Hollywood has seen in recent decades.

Psychological Abuse: The Power of Control

Throughout their relationship, Kim endured years of psychological abuse at the hands of Diddy — a form of control as insidious as it is devastating. In her diaries, Kim wrote with anguish about how Diddy expertly manipulated her emotions, making her dependent on him even when she was aware of the harm he was causing.

This manipulation was not only emotional but extended to control over her social and professional life. Diddy was a figure of immense power, and he used that power to isolate Kim, keeping her from pursuing her dreams and binding her to him. In her writings, Kim frequently mentioned feeling like she was imprisoned in a gilded cage—surrounded by luxury but deprived of the freedom to chart her own future.

The relationship between Kim and Diddy was characterized by toxic dynamics. Kim often described how he would oscillate between moments of tenderness and affection and periods of cold distance or anger, turning the relationship into an emotional rollercoaster that kept her in a constant state of uncertainty. "You never know where you stand with him," Kim wrote in one entry, "one moment he loves you, the next you feel invisible."

Infidelity and Public Humiliation

One of the most devastating aspects of Kim's relationship with Diddy, as recounted in her diaries, was his repeated infidelity. Not only did Diddy cheat on Kim with other women, but he often did so in such a public manner that his affairs became common knowledge through the media. The birth of a daughter from another relationship was just one of many events that deeply shook Kim's mental health.

Kim frequently wrote about the pain caused by these betrayals and the overwhelming sense of humiliation she felt, especially as their relationship was constantly under the public eye. "Every time I read about him with another woman, it breaks me inside," Kim wrote. Yet, despite everything, she remained tied to Diddy, unable to break free from that spiral of emotional dependency.

Diddy's infidelities were not only a personal affront to Kim but also a form of psychological abuse. He knew that each betrayal would further weaken Kim, reinforcing his control over her. The way Diddy handled these situations — often minimizing the impact of his actions — contributed to an environment where Kim felt increasingly insecure and vulnerable.

Physical Abuse: The Dark Side Behind Closed Doors

While the emotional abuse was deeply ingrained in their relationship, Kim revealed in her diaries instances of physical abuse as well. According to her writings, Diddy had violent outbursts during which he didn't hesitate to be physically aggressive. Though these episodes weren't frequent, they left deep marks on Kim — both physically and emotionally.

In one particularly harrowing episode described in her writings, Kim recounted a furious argument that escalated into physical violence. "I felt like I had been erased," Kim wrote. "Like my existence meant nothing to him." These moments were often followed by apologies and promises of change — typical cycles in abusive relationships that made it difficult for Kim to find the strength to leave Diddy for good.

The accusations of physical abuse against Diddy represent one of the most severe aspects of Kim's revelations. Until then, there had been no public accusations linking him to acts of physical violence, which made these claims all the more shocking. Now, with the ongoing investigation, these accusations are being carefully examined by authorities, as new testimonies from people close to the couple continue to emerge.

Power Dynamics and Financial Control

One of the most complex aspects of the relationship between Kim and Diddy was the imbalance of financial power. With a fortune estimated in the hundreds of millions of dollars, Diddy held total control over the couple's finances. This financial disparity translated into even broader control over Kim's decisions, both in her personal and professional life.

In her diaries, Kim described how Diddy would frequently use money as a tool of manipulation. When she attempted to distance herself or make independent decisions, Diddy would remind her that everything they had—from their luxurious home to the clothes she wore—was thanks to him. This left her in a position of dependence, forced to make compromises for the sake of their children and her own financial security.

The Legal Implications of the Revelations

With the discovery of Kim's diaries and the testimonies that followed, Diddy's situation has become increasingly complicated from a legal perspective. The accusations of emotional and physical abuse, combined with revelations about his ties to sex trafficking, have led to the opening of federal investigations. Kim's diaries, although private, have become a key piece of evidence in the case against Diddy, and their contents are being closely analyzed by investigators and attorneys to determine if there is sufficient ground for charges in court.

The investigation has also expanded to include other figures close to Diddy, with the goal of understanding if there was a system of complicity that allowed the abuse to continue unchecked for years. The inquiry is not limited to the personal abuses Kim endured, but also explores allegations of sex trafficking and exploitation involving other women. If these accusations are confirmed, the scandal could have devastating consequences not only for Diddy but for the entire entertainment industry.

Chapter 4: Hollywood Under the Microscope

A Culture of Power and Silence

Hollywood—the industry that has built dreams and transformed ordinary people into global icons—has always had a dark side. Behind the lights, red carpets, and awards, there exists a deeply ingrained culture of power abuse, silence, and control. The scandal involving Sean "Diddy" Combs and Kim Porter is not an anomaly but rather another example of how power is manipulated to protect those at the top, while hiding uncomfortable truths.

The Diddy-Porter case has resurfaced a pattern that we've seen before with scandals like those involving Harvey Weinstein, Bill Cosby, and many others. Celebrities, thanks to their fame and wealth, are often shielded from accusations that could destroy their careers. This system of protection creates an environment where victims like Kim Porter feel trapped, unable to speak out or seek justice.

An Industry Built on Silence

One of the most disturbing aspects of the entertainment industry is the code of silence surrounding powerful figures. Celebrities like Diddy, with their vast economic control and influence, don't just wield power over those who work for them—they are also supported by those who are supposed to safeguard justice. Agents, lawyers, producers, and even journalists often act as accomplices, turning a blind eye or actively protecting the stars for personal gain or fear of professional retaliation.

The case of Kim Porter highlights just how dangerous this dynamic can be. Even when the evidence of abuse is clear and detailed, as in her diaries, victims face an impenetrable wall of silence. Kim lived for years under Diddy's control, never feeling free to speak out, fearing the consequences for her life and that of her children. The fear of losing financial stability and being labeled as a "troublemaker" in Hollywood's tight-knit circles forced her into silence for far too long.

The Weinstein Scandal and the Turning Point of #MeToo

The #MeToo movement, which began gaining momentum in 2017, shook Hollywood like no other event in recent decades. For the first time, women in the industry began speaking openly about the abuse they had suffered at the hands of powerful producers, directors, and actors. The most emblematic case is that of Harvey Weinstein, who for years used his power to sexually harass and assault women—many of whom were too afraid to speak out for fear of career retaliation.

Weinstein was protected for decades by a network of complicity and fear, much like Diddy. Although the two cases are different, there is an underlying similarity: the absolute power these figures held over those who depended on them. Testimonies from women like Ashley Judd and Rose McGowan revealed a system that not only tolerated but encouraged silence. This pattern repeats in Kim Porter's case, as she endured Diddy's abuses in silence for years, knowing that speaking out could jeopardize her safety and that of her children.

The #MeToo movement has allowed many women in Hollywood to break their silence, but it has also shown how difficult it is to achieve justice in an industry so focused on maintaining an image of perfection. Despite progress since 2017, the industry remains deeply conservative when it comes to protecting its most powerful members.

Abuse of Power and Media Influence

One of the most powerful tools at celebrities' disposal is their control over the media. Thanks to their connections and influence, they are often able to manipulate the narratives that appear in newspapers and on television. For years, the press treated the relationship between Kim Porter and Diddy as a simple tale of "ups and downs," never delving into the real issues hiding behind the facade. This is yet another example of how the Hollywood system shields its powerful.

The media not only minimizes the abuse but often reinforces the positive public image of stars. Diddy, for instance, has long been portrayed as a successful entrepreneur, a family man, and a philanthropist. This control over his public image has been crucial in allowing him to continue abusing his power without facing consequences. Only with the release of Kim's diaries and the subsequent involvement of authorities has the truth started to come to light.

The Difficulty for Hollywood Victims to Seek Justice

Another crucial aspect to consider is the immense difficulty victims face when trying to seek justice in a legal system that often favors the powerful. In many cases, victims of sexual or psychological abuse in Hollywood are discouraged from pursuing legal action due to the high costs, threats of retaliation, and the potential ruin of their careers.

Kim Porter never openly accused Diddy of the abuse she suffered — likely due to this very dynamic. She knew that going public could have meant the end of her public life and financial ruin. Additionally, victims of powerful celebrities like Diddy are often subject to smear campaigns, legal threats, and psychological pressure to stay silent. Even when they choose to speak out, they face a long, arduous battle to obtain justice.

The Weinstein case has shown that even with overwhelming evidence, securing a conviction is not simple. The same applies to Diddy, who now faces not only the accusations made by Kim Porter but also the possibility of other accusations coming to light during the investigation. However, the road to justice is long and full of obstacles, and his immense wealth and influence could play a crucial role in his defense.

A Cultural Shift on the Horizon?

Despite the resistance to change, the Diddy-Porter scandal could mark a significant turning point for Hollywood. Like the Weinstein case, this scandal could push the industry to seriously reflect on its internal dynamics and how it treats victims of abuse. However, the larger question remains: will Hollywood truly be able to reform, or will it continue to protect the powerful at the expense of the vulnerable?

Many stars, after Kim Porter's death and the subsequent revelations, have started expressing their support for victims of abuse and calling for change in the industry. The hope is that, with more testimonies and revelations, a safer environment can be created where victims feel empowered to speak out and seek justice without fear of retaliation.

Chapter 5: The Public and Media Reaction

The Immediate Impact of the Revelations

When the first details of the Kim Porter and Sean "Diddy" Combs case surfaced, the world of entertainment and the media was hit with a fresh wave of shock and outrage. The revelations from Kim's diaries stunned not only the couple's fans but also the wider public, who had already been grappling with an industry increasingly marred by scandals of abuse and corruption.

The media, in particular, played a crucial role in amplifying these revelations. From gossip outlets like *TMZ* to more respected publications like *The New York Times* and *The Guardian*, everyone covered the Diddy-Porter case. However, the tone and perspectives adopted varied greatly, reflecting the complex web of economic and media interests at play.

The Initial Reactions: Between Shock and Skepticism

When the story of Kim Porter first broke, the public's reaction was one of disbelief. Most people knew Kim solely as the mother of Diddy's children—a figure on the periphery of the music mogul's massive fame. The accusations of emotional and physical abuse, along with the revelations from her diaries, suddenly transformed Diddy's public image from a successful entrepreneur and philanthropist into that of a potential abuser.

However, as often happens with high-profile celebrities, not everyone was quick to believe the allegations. Diddy's most loyal fans rushed to his defense, calling the accusations "fabrications" or "exaggerations" aimed at tearing down his career. Some media outlets, particularly those with close ties to the entertainment world, initially adopted a cautious stance, refraining from making strong comments until the investigation yielded more concrete evidence.

At this stage, the narrative was split: on one side were those demanding justice for Kim and other Hollywood victims, and on the other, those who defended Diddy's public image, unwilling to believe that someone so influential could be guilty of such serious crimes.

Diddy's Crisis Management

As one might expect from a figure of Diddy's caliber, he reacted swiftly to the scandal. Aware of the devastating potential of the accusations, Diddy immediately enlisted his legal and PR teams to respond and control the public narrative. His strategy, at least initially, was to categorically deny all allegations, describing them as false and baseless.

Diddy also relied on his powerful media contacts to minimize the impact of the revelations. Several media outlets and journalists close to the star began publishing articles questioning the authenticity of Kim Porter's diaries, casting doubt on the legitimacy of the allegations. At the same time, Diddy kept a high public profile, continuing to attend social and philanthropic events to project an image of a man unshaken by the scandal.

This crisis management strategy was a classic example of how celebrities with vast PR resources try to control the public narrative in order to protect their image. However, the scale of the accusations and the intensifying investigations have made it increasingly difficult for Diddy to maintain total control of the story.

The Role of Social Media: A Narrative Out of Control

With the rise of social media, traditional methods of controlling media narratives have become far less effective. Platforms like Twitter, Instagram, TikTok, and Facebook exploded with discussions about the case, with millions of users sharing their opinions. While traditional media adopted a neutral tone and waited for the investigation to develop, social media became a battlefield of conflicting opinions.

Hashtags like #JusticeForKimPorter and #DiddyAbuse went viral, driven by social justice movements and growing public discussions about celebrity power. The younger generation, in particular, quickly aligned with Kim, viewing her not just as a victim of abuse but as a symbol of the countless women who have suffered violence and oppression in the entertainment industry.

Social media played a critical role in keeping the scandal alive. Even when traditional media outlets began to shift their focus, the public continued to discuss, share, and create content related to Kim Porter's story. This constant online conversation made it much harder for Diddy and his PR team to suppress the story or steer public opinion in their favor.

Celebrities and Hollywood's Divided Response

The Kim Porter case also deeply divided Hollywood. Some celebrities, such as Taraji P. Henson and Gabrielle Union, openly supported the victims of abuse, using their platforms to express solidarity and call for justice for Kim. These public shows of support had a significant impact on the public's perception, demonstrating that even Hollywood's most influential figures were willing to take a stand for the truth.

On the other hand, many of Diddy's friends and collaborators remained conspicuously silent. This silence reflected the complexities of relationships within the entertainment industry, where alliances and professional ties often influence who takes a stance and who stays on the sidelines. Several key figures in the music and film industries chose not to comment, fearing the repercussions of damaging their relationships with such a powerful figure as Diddy.

However, as the public pressure mounted and the accusations gained traction, even those who had initially stayed silent began to face scrutiny.

The Role of Streaming and Entertainment Platforms

Another crucial aspect of the public reaction to the Diddy-Porter case was the role of entertainment platforms like Spotify, Apple Music, and YouTube. In recent years, there has been growing debate about how these platforms should handle artists accused of serious crimes. In the case of R. Kelly, for example, many streaming platforms limited the promotion of his music following sexual abuse accusations.

With Diddy, a similar debate emerged: should these platforms continue to promote his music in light of such serious allegations? While no drastic decisions were made initially, the discussion gained momentum, with many users calling for the removal or limitation of Diddy's songs as the investigation progressed.

Chapter 6: The Social Implications of the Scandal

The Diddy-Porter Case: A Mirror for Society

The scandal involving Sean "Diddy" Combs and Kim Porter is more than just a matter of personal dynamics or legal accusations. The revelations about the alleged abuse are not an isolated event; this scandal reflects broader trends and issues within society, particularly regarding the treatment of women, the power of celebrities, and the impunity of those who control economic and media empires.

The social implications of this scandal go far beyond Hollywood. The accusations against Diddy shine a light on issues of gender inequality, power abuse, and how society protects (or ignores) toxic and abusive behavior in powerful people. The fact that Kim Porter, despite her proximity to fame and fortune, remained silent for years illustrates how difficult it is for abuse victims to speak out and seek justice, even when they are in privileged environments.

The Role of the #MeToo Movement

The #MeToo movement has been central in raising awareness about sexual and power abuses across traditionally male-dominated industries. Launched in 2006 and growing exponentially after the Weinstein case in 2017, #MeToo gave a voice to thousands of women (and men) who had suffered abuse but had never had the opportunity—or courage—to speak out before.

The Diddy-Kim Porter case clearly falls under the #MeToo umbrella. Kim is one of many women who, though in a seemingly privileged position, found herself trapped in an abusive relationship with a man who controlled not only her personal life but also her career and public image. Her decision not to publicly accuse Diddy during her lifetime is understandable within a context where victims are often doubted, ignored, or even punished for daring to challenge a powerful figure.

The accusations that emerge from her diaries, however, fit perfectly into the cultural transformation inspired by #MeToo. Even after her death, her story holds the power to influence public discussion, helping to create a safer space for abuse victims, particularly those silenced for years by unequal power dynamics.

The Power of Celebrity and the Impunity of the Elite

One of the key themes emerging from this scandal is how celebrity power can protect behaviors that would be unacceptable for ordinary people. Hollywood and the music industry stars are surrounded by legal teams, managers, PR professionals, and media support systems that defend them at all costs. This structure creates a barrier, making it difficult — if not impossible — for victims to achieve justice.

In Diddy's case, his enormous wealth and control over the music industry allowed him to avoid facing serious accusations for years, despite signs of problematic behavior. Even before Kim's diaries surfaced, rumors of abuse and manipulation had circulated. However, as in many cases, these accusations weren't taken seriously, either by the media or those close to Diddy.

The impunity of celebrities is a recurring theme in many power abuse scandals. When influential figures like Diddy, Bill Cosby, or Harvey Weinstein are accused of crimes, they often manage to avoid serious consequences due to the financial resources and political connections they have accumulated over time. This not only protects the abuser but also creates an environment where victims feel even more isolated and powerless.

Gender Inequality and Power

The Diddy-Porter scandal highlights the deep-seated gender inequality that persists not only in Hollywood but across society. Kim Porter, despite being an independent woman and a loving mother, found herself trapped in a relationship where power was heavily skewed in her partner's favor. This power imbalance is common in abusive relationships, where the victim often feels incapable of leaving or reporting the abuse, especially if they depend financially or socially on the abuser.

In a culture like Hollywood, where image is everything and public relations play a critical role in one's career, women are particularly vulnerable to these power imbalances. Kim's choice to remain silent for so long wasn't just a reflection of her personal relationship with Diddy but also of the broader gender dynamics in society. Women are often taught to endure, protect their families, and sacrifice their own well-being for the sake of others—especially when children are involved.

The Social Lesson of the Scandal

The Diddy-Porter scandal is not just an example of personal abuse but a warning to society at large. The dynamics of control and manipulation that characterized Kim and Diddy's relationship are not unique to the world of celebrities. They reflect the power dynamics in many everyday relationships, whether in the workplace, romantic partnerships, or family settings.

One of the most important lessons we can learn from this case is the need to create safe spaces for abuse victims. This involves not just offering legal and psychological support but also changing the cultural narrative around victims, dismantling the prejudices that continue to blame them or see them as weak.

Kim Porter's story is a powerful reminder of how damaging abusive relationships can be and of how necessary it is to continue fighting for justice and equality. Her voice, finally heard through her diaries, can inspire other women to break their silence and seek the support they deserve.

A Cultural Transformation and the Future of Hollywood

As with the Weinstein case, the Diddy-Porter scandal could mark a turning point for Hollywood and the entertainment industry. The growing public awareness and social pressure from movements like #MeToo are pushing the industry to reevaluate its internal dynamics. More and more people are taking a stand against power abuse, and companies are implementing stricter policies to ensure the safety and respect of all workers.

Still, the road to a fairer Hollywood is long. The power structures that have protected figures like Diddy for decades do not disappear easily. But the Diddy-Porter scandal shows us that things are changing and that the voices of victims, even when long silenced, can still have a lasting impact.

Chapter 7: The Consequences for Sean Combs and His Empire

Diddy Under Siege: The Fall of a Legend

When the scandal surrounding Sean "Diddy" Combs began to unfold, the consequences were swift and far-reaching. Diddy, one of the most influential figures in the music and entertainment industry, suddenly found himself under intense scrutiny for reasons entirely different from those that had built his legacy. The image of the successful businessman, philanthropist, and family man that he had carefully crafted over the years was quickly tarnished by allegations of abuse and manipulation. But what does all this mean for his empire? And what does the future hold for a man who once stood at the pinnacle of success?

Financial Repercussions

One of the first tangible consequences of the scandal was its financial impact. Diddy sits atop a multimillion-dollar empire that spans far beyond the music industry—encompassing fashion, restaurants, and alcoholic beverages. His vodka brand *Cîroc* and his tequila brand *DeLeón* have been major sources of revenue, along with his record labels and other business ventures. However, the scandal has put many of these partnerships at risk.

In recent years, we've seen how businesses react quickly to scandals involving celebrities, especially when accusations of abuse arise. In the case of R. Kelly, for example, many streaming platforms like Spotify and Apple Music limited the promotion of his music, while several business partners severed ties with him. In Diddy's case, companies associated with him will have to make difficult decisions about how to manage their collaborations.

Initial responses from Diddy's business partners have been cautious. Companies like *Diageo*, which distributes *Cîroc*, have been under increasing public pressure to take a firm stance on the scandal. For these companies, the issue isn't just legal—it's also reputational. Associating with a figure involved in such a scandal could irreparably damage their brand, especially in an era when consumers demand more accountability and social responsibility from the companies they support.

His Music Career: An Icon in Decline?

Diddy is widely regarded as one of the most influential figures in hip-hop history. From founding *Bad Boy Records* in the '90s, he helped launch the careers of legendary artists like *The Notorious B.I.G.*, *Faith Evans*, and *Mase*. As both a producer and artist, Diddy was behind some of the most iconic tracks of recent decades. But this scandal could put his entire musical legacy at risk.

The music industry relies heavily on public image. If an artist or producer becomes embroiled in scandal, it can directly affect sales and success. Diddy built his music empire on his ability to connect with audiences, but these allegations could alienate many fans, particularly younger listeners who have grown up in an era more sensitive to issues of gender rights and power dynamics.

However, the music world is notoriously fickle and often quick to forgive, as seen in previous cases. Artists like *Chris Brown*, despite being involved in serious scandals, have managed to maintain prolific careers. The question for Diddy is whether the public and the music industry will be willing to forgive him, or whether this scandal will mark the end of his artistic and business career.

Legal Consequences: What Does Diddy Risk?

Beyond the financial and professional fallout, Diddy faces potentially devastating legal consequences. The accusations of emotional, physical, and psychological abuse found in Kim Porter's diaries, if substantiated, could lead to multiple lawsuits. Beyond the damage to his image, Diddy could be staring at years of legal battles that could threaten his future.

In the United States, laws concerning abuse and domestic violence are strict, and if the allegations are supported by solid evidence, Diddy could face a slew of civil and criminal cases. Already, as the scandal unfolded, there were reports of lawyers representing other potential victims preparing lawsuits against him. These cases could involve multimillion-dollar compensation claims, which could significantly erode his vast fortune.

Moreover, the allegations of sex trafficking are particularly grave. If federal investigations were to find Diddy involved in trafficking or exploitation, as some accusations suggest, the legal consequences would be even more severe. Recent cases like those of *Jeffrey Epstein* and *Ghislaine Maxwell* show that the US justice system is becoming increasingly intolerant of such offenses, and if these accusations prove true, Diddy could face long-term legal ramifications.

PR Management: A High-Stakes Defense

Like many other powerful figures who have been caught in scandals of this magnitude, Diddy quickly mobilized a team of legal and PR experts to manage the crisis. His strategy so far has been to categorically deny all allegations, using a tone that portrays the revelations as false or exaggerated. However, this defense carries significant risk. Should more victims come forward with concrete evidence, Diddy's defense could crumble under the weight of these accusations, causing irreversible damage to his reputation and career.

Diddy's PR team is also working to shift the public's attention away from the allegations by focusing on his philanthropic work and positive projects. Throughout his career, Diddy has emphasized his role as a philanthropist, supporting causes related to the Black community and urban development. However, today's public is much more critical and aware, and these distraction tactics may not be enough to salvage his image.

Personal Repercussions: The Future of His Family

As Diddy grapples with the enormous public and legal pressure, we must not overlook the impact this scandal has had on his family. Throughout his career, Diddy has emphasized his role as a devoted father, and his children have often been at the center of his public life. But the abuse accusations cast a shadow over his image as a loving, present parent.

Kim Porter's children, especially the twin daughters, have been deeply affected by their mother's death and the revelations that followed. Beyond their personal pain, they now face the harsh reality of the accusations against their father. This scandal is likely to affect their lives for years to come, both emotionally and legally, and they will likely need substantial support to cope with the consequences of what has unfolded.

Diddy's social network—his friends and industry colleagues—will also be tested. Some may choose to distance themselves from him to protect their own careers, while others may remain loyal. However, his family dynamics will undoubtedly be among the most complex challenges he faces in the long term.

Chapter 8: The Future of Hollywood and Kim Porter's Legacy

Hollywood After the Scandal: A New Beginning or the Same Old Patterns?

The scandal involving Sean "Diddy" Combs and Kim Porter has sent shockwaves through Hollywood and the broader entertainment industry. Yet, the crucial question remains: Will this scandal truly represent a turning point for the industry, or will it simply become another dark chapter that is soon forgotten?

In recent years, we have seen several similar scandals expose the darker side of power in Hollywood. The #MeToo movement and cases involving figures like Harvey Weinstein, Bill Cosby, and others have highlighted how deeply rooted power abuse is in the industry. However, despite the visibility of these scandals, the structural changes promised have been slow and, in many cases, superficial.

The Role of Hollywood's Institutions

One of the key factors in shaping Hollywood's future will be how its major institutions respond to this scandal. Big production companies, talent agencies, and distribution platforms all play a role in deciding who gets promoted, protected, or sidelined. After the Weinstein scandal, many of these institutions vowed to overhaul their internal policies to combat abuse and ensure a safer work environment for everyone.

However, as the Diddy-Porter case demonstrates, there is still much work to be done. The impunity enjoyed by some of the biggest stars in the industry proves that until these institutions take a firm stand against abuse, meaningful change will remain elusive. Hollywood has a long history of protecting its stars—especially those who generate enormous profits—and the battle between ethics and revenue will be one of the major challenges in the coming years.

Cultural Change in Progress: Is There Hope?

Despite Hollywood's reluctance to fully embrace change, there is a cultural shift that cannot be ignored. Social media, growing public awareness, and the power of collective voices have transformed the way the Diddy-Porter scandal (and others like it) is perceived and discussed. Today's public is far less willing to turn a blind eye to power abuse, and the once-untouchable stars now find themselves increasingly accountable for their actions.

The #MeToo movement triggered a significant cultural transformation, pushing many women and men to openly share their experiences of abuse. This has created a climate of increased responsibility, where behaviors that were once accepted or ignored are no longer tolerated. However, it's also true that the path toward full transformation is still long. Hollywood, like many other industries, tends to be conservative when it comes to dismantling its established power structures.

The reactions to Kim Porter's death and the subsequent revelations in her diaries show that the public is ready for a deeper reflection. This is not just about a single case of abuse but a symptom of a systemic problem. Whether Hollywood will take these issues seriously depends on the willingness of those in power to make difficult decisions and be prepared to sacrifice short-term profits in favor of a more just and inclusive culture.

Kim Porter's Legacy: A Silent Voice That Still Speaks

As we focus on the legal and cultural consequences of the scandal, it's important not to lose sight of Kim Porter's legacy. Kim was not just a victim in this story but a complex figure, a woman who fought to maintain control over her life and family despite personal challenges. Her diaries, which were made public only after her death, serve as a powerful testament to her courage and resilience.

Her decision to write about her experiences, perhaps to protect her children or to find emotional relief, has allowed many other women to see their own stories reflected. Kim was a mother, a model, and a person who struggled to balance her private life with the complexities of being in a relationship with such a powerful public figure. Through her writings, she gave a voice to those women who have felt trapped in toxic relationships, where power and control overshadow love and respect.

Her story has sparked a broader conversation about how the entertainment industry and society treat victims of abuse, how power can be used to manipulate and control, and how even those closest to celebrities can suffer in silence.

The Broader Lessons: Power Dynamics in Relationships

The Diddy-Porter scandal offers an opportunity to reflect not only on the abuse dynamics within Hollywood but also on the broader power relationships in society. One of the most important lessons we can draw from this case is that power, when concentrated in the hands of a few, can easily be abused. People who accumulate immense wealth and a vast network of professional and personal relationships often feel invulnerable, believing they can act without consequences.

However, the events of recent years, with scandals involving people like Weinstein, Epstein, and now Diddy, show that the era of impunity is coming to an end. More and more people are realizing that even the most powerful individuals can and should be held accountable for their actions, and this is a positive sign for the future.

Power dynamics, both personal and professional, need to be rethought and rebalanced. Companies and institutions must do more to protect vulnerable people within their systems, and abusive dynamics must be addressed with transparency and seriousness. Hollywood has the potential to become a model of change for other industries, showing that it's possible to create an environment where everyone — regardless of status — is treated with respect and dignity.

Extra Chapter 1: Whispered Stories and Dark Secrets

The Hidden World of Hollywood: Who Knew What?

Hollywood has long been known for its ability to craft illusions and hide its darkest secrets. Behind the glamour and fame, some stories are whispered but rarely see the light of day. For years, insiders in the entertainment industry claimed that the tumultuous relationship between Sean "Diddy" Combs and Kim Porter was no secret to those closest to them. Numerous sources have suggested that rumors of manipulation and emotional abuse had been circulating for years, though no one dared to speak out publicly. Discussions about their troubled relationship were a common subject at exclusive Hollywood parties, but these conversations seldom left the private circles of the rich and powerful.

According to a former associate of Diddy, who has chosen to remain anonymous, tensions between the couple were already obvious by 2005, around the time of the success of one of Diddy's major releases from *Bad Boy Records*. During a lavish party in Miami, Kim allegedly confronted Diddy in front of close friends, accusing him of having an affair with an up-and-coming singer. Witnesses recall that the argument became so heated that several attendees had to step in to prevent the confrontation from escalating further.

The Miami Mansion: A Center for Excess and Secrets

Another story emerging from insiders close to the family concerns one of Diddy's mansions in Miami, which allegedly served as the backdrop for extravagant and secretive parties. Within the luxurious confines of this mansion, events were held that attracted some of the biggest names in music and Hollywood. However, behind the facade of glitz and glamour were tales of power struggles, secret relationships, and emotional abuse.

Despite being the public partner of one of the music industry's biggest moguls, Kim Porter was often marginalized during these events, sidelined as Diddy's celebrity status took center stage. According to people familiar with the situation, Kim privately confided in a close friend, expressing feelings of being trapped in what she referred to as "a golden cage." While she enjoyed the luxurious lifestyle that came with being Diddy's partner, she also felt suffocated by the control he exerted over her personal and professional life.

Other Hidden Relationships: Diddy's Web of Secrets

Though Diddy's numerous affairs were often a topic of public speculation, several of his secret relationships were reportedly kept well under wraps through skillful management and strict non-disclosure agreements. Insiders within the entertainment industry have suggested that at least three prominent singers and actresses had brief but significant relationships with Diddy, none of which ever made it into the public spotlight due to meticulous planning and PR interventions.

One of these rumored relationships involved a globally famous pop star during the early 2000s. According to whispers in Hollywood, a paparazzo once managed to snap photos of Diddy and this star in a compromising situation. However, the photos were swiftly bought and destroyed before they could ever make their way to the public. This ensured that both Diddy and the other celebrity could avoid a damaging scandal.

A Possible Connection to Jeffrey Epstein?

Perhaps one of the most unsettling rumors that has surfaced in relation to Diddy is his alleged connection to Jeffrey Epstein, the notorious financier convicted of sex trafficking minors. While no direct evidence has ever surfaced tying Diddy to Epstein's criminal activities, there have long been whispers of a friendship between the two men, with Diddy reportedly attending some of Epstein's infamous parties at his opulent estates.

Some witnesses claim that Diddy was a regular guest at Epstein's lavish events during the early 2000s, where the social elite would gather in secrecy. It is said that Kim was aware of these gatherings, and that Epstein's influence was a source of deep conflict between her and Diddy. Though no concrete proof has emerged linking Diddy to the darker elements of Epstein's life, the persistent rumors continue to cast a shadow over his already damaged reputation.

Extra Chapter 2: Hollywood Gossip and Power Intrigue

The Untold Love Triangle: Diddy, Kim, and a Famous Actor

Another hidden story that has been circulating within Hollywood's tight-knit circles for years involves a rumored love triangle between Diddy, Kim Porter, and one of the industry's most famous actors. The name of this actor, if revealed, could shock the public. According to internal sources, Kim became romantically involved with this actor during one of her periods of separation from Diddy between 2006 and 2007.

The actor, known for being one of Hollywood's top A-listers, is said to have dated Kim for several months, during which the two were spotted together at exclusive locations. However, when Diddy discovered the relationship, he allegedly intervened directly, threatening the actor and ensuring that the romance came to an abrupt end. It is believed that to avoid a scandal, the actor agreed to cut ties with Kim, fearing the potential damage to his career. This event, kept under wraps for years, was reportedly one of the key factors contributing to Kim's emotional struggles during that time.

A Secret Legal Battle: Deals Behind the Scenes

Another lesser-known aspect of the relationship between Kim and Diddy revolves around the secret legal agreements negotiated throughout their time together. While the public saw a couple who reconciled and separated periodically, behind the scenes, a complex legal battle was brewing over financial control and custody of their children.

Sources close to the couple have revealed that, shortly before Kim's death, she consulted one of Los Angeles' most influential attorneys to discuss the possibility of filing for full custody of the twins. Kim was reportedly exhausted by Diddy's influence over their lives and wanted to regain control of her and her children's future. However, this plan was tragically cut short by her sudden death, leaving many questions about her true intentions unresolved.

Lost Documents and Hidden Truths

Another rumor fueling conspiracy theories concerns certain legal documents that Kim Porter allegedly prepared in the months leading up to her death. These documents, rumored to contain explosive revelations about Diddy, included details of secret financial agreements and alleged abuses. According to one insider, these critical papers mysteriously disappeared after Kim's death, raising suspicions that someone might have intentionally removed them to protect Diddy's reputation. If true, this story could shed further light on the power dynamics between the two and how Diddy maintained control over Kim, even as she tried to distance herself.

Conclusions

The Entertainment Industry Under Fire

The scandal that has engulfed Sean "Diddy" Combs, centered around the posthumous revelations of Kim Porter, is much more than just an isolated case. It serves as a window into the often-hidden realities of power, abuse, and control within personal and professional relationships, especially in the entertainment industry. It's a story that shines a light on universal themes of inequality, enforced silence, and impunity — issues that resonate not only in Hollywood but in any environment where power is disproportionately concentrated.

The Entertainment Industry on Trial

One of the key lessons that emerges from this case is the critical role power dynamics play within the entertainment industry. Hollywood has long been built on myths of success, fame, and fortune, but behind the glittering surface lie stories of control, exploitation, and abuse. As shown by past scandals, such as those involving Harvey Weinstein and R. Kelly, celebrities who reach positions of influence often enjoy extraordinary protection. They are surrounded by legal teams, PR firms, and media outlets working tirelessly to shield them from their wrongdoings and mitigate any fallout from their actions.

The Diddy-Porter case is no different. The revelations in Kim Porter's diaries reveal how even those closest to powerful figures can become victims of invisible abuse, trapped in relationships where emotional and financial dependency makes it nearly impossible to speak out. The code of silence that surrounds such cases is not an isolated problem; it is a symptom of a system designed to protect the powerful at the expense of the vulnerable. The challenge Hollywood faces in the coming years will be demonstrating that meaningful change is possible, transforming into an industry that rewards talent and creativity — not abuse and manipulation.

The Courage of Victims and Kim Porter's Role

Kim Porter, though she never publicly accused Diddy during her life, left behind an indelible mark through her diaries. Her decision to document her experiences, even in private, has allowed her voice to be heard after her passing, breaking the silence that surrounded her for years. Her testimony serves as a powerful reminder of the courage required to tell one's story, particularly when entangled with a figure as powerful as Diddy.

Kim represents countless women who have endured cruel and suffocating realities behind closed doors. Her desire to protect her children and maintain a facade of family stability forced her to remain in a toxic and damaging relationship for far too long. Her contribution, through the words she left behind, will be remembered not just as an act of personal resilience but as a testimony that will continue to inspire other women to speak up and seek justice.

Broader Lessons for Society

The implications of the Diddy-Porter case extend far beyond the world of celebrities. Gender inequality, financial control, and psychological manipulation are issues that affect many people across the globe. Though Hollywood is an exceptionally visible environment, the power dynamics and abuse patterns revealed in this case are present in many other industries and social settings.

The most important takeaway from this case is the need for systemic and cultural reforms. Abuse victims—regardless of their social or economic status—must feel safe in speaking out about their experiences without fear of retaliation or isolation. We must continue to support movements like #MeToo, which have paved the way for crucial conversations about power abuse, and we must work to create an environment where victims are heard and believed.

The Diddy-Porter case reminds us that while power can be used to oppress and silence, there are also tools and platforms available to bring truth to light and fight against injustice. Legal reforms, transparent investigations, and support for victims are essential steps toward a more equitable and just society.

Looking Forward: A New Hollywood?

The case of Kim Porter and Sean "Diddy" Combs represents a potential turning point for Hollywood, but the question that remains is whether this scandal will truly lead to lasting change. In recent years, Hollywood has been forced to confront its darkest realities, and while some progress has been made, there is still much work to be done. The power structures that have shielded figures like Diddy for decades are not easy to dismantle, but the growing social pressure and public awareness are pushing the industry in a more just direction.

Hollywood has the opportunity to become a beacon of change for other industries, but this will require concrete and sustained effort. Stricter policies must be introduced to prevent abuses, and victims must be protected and supported. Only then can we speak of true transformation. Kim Porter has offered society a chance — to reflect, act, and change. Her legacy is not just one of a woman who suffered, but of a voice that, even in silence, spoke for those who never had the strength or opportunity to do so.

Made in the USA
Columbia, SC
28 September 2024

43191901R00037